Time's Up!

Harry Andrews finally got the perfect scam done! He was living his dream life! He knew there was a time limit on the dream. It was now. Was he ready to go forward, or would he stagnate right there?

Contents

About the author

CD Moulton has traveled extensively over much of the world both in the music business, where he was a rock guitarist, songwriter and arranger and in an import/export business. He has been everything from a bar owner to auto salvage (junkyard) manager, longshoreman to high steel worker, orchid grower to landscaper, tropical fish farmer to commercial fisherman. He started writing books in 1983 and has published more than 350 books as of January 1, 2023. His most popular books to date are about research with orchids, though much of his science fiction and fantasy work has proven popular. He wrote the CD Grimes, PI series, and the Det. Nick Storie series, Clint Faraday series, and many other works.

He now resides in Gualaca, Chiriqui, Panamá, where he writes books, plays music with friends, does research with orchids and medicinal plants. He has lately become involved in fighting for the rights of the indigenous people, who are among his closest friends, and in fighting the extreme corruption in the courts and police in Panamá.

He offers the free e-book, *Fading Paradise*, that explains what he has been through because of the corruption.

CD is the discoverer of the Chadam Protocol for curing cancer.

Facebook page Ambrosia peruviana for cancer.

<u>*Glorious Sunrise*</u>

Harry Andrews sighed and rolled over to stare out the window to the beach. It was a glorious sunrise. He was looking directly east out of that window.

Life was great! For the past seven years, it was a dream realized!

He had lived a hard earlier life. His mother was a drunk and his father a drunk and coke freak. His brother was in the pen for twenty to life, his sister had run off at sixteen with a motorcycle bum and had been killed in a "suspicious" accident two months later. It turned out her boyfriend had two former girlfriends who had accidents when they got sick of him and started arguing all the time.

"Snake" Patterson. He got beat to death just three weeks later, when the cousin of the second girlfriend found him in a bar in Fresno, California. It was ruled self-defense. Several other bikers said Bill Arnold, the cousin, had merely come in for a beer and was talking with Patterson, then Patterson suddenly hit Arnold in the face. Arnold, a much smaller man, but one who held a third degree black belt in some kind of karate, made short work of Patterson, who died from internal injuries in intense pain fourteen hours later.

So far as Harry was concerned, justice was served. The world was rid of a piece of societal garbage.

Anyhow, Harry's parents had died in a plane crash just a bit more than nine years ago. Harry was just seventeen, and suddenly on his own. He inherited a little rundown house in a suburb of Los Angeles. His only skill was shoplifting and a natural flare for mechanics.

He lived in the house for two years, mainly by shoplifting more expensive items and working when called for an auto repair shop. A very upper-end auto repair shop. Masseratis, Lambourginis, Vipers, Lexus, etc. He got the work because he had a talent where he could listen to an engine and instantly tell exactly what wasn't perfect. He was able to make parts where there were none in stock by adapting other models.

He learned a bit about scams there, too.

"Buzz" Bertoni was a very skilled scam artist. He was a likeable sort, who you automatically trusted. He put his scams together with attention to details, so he always had a way out. He warned Harry to never work a scam on anyone who couldn't afford it.

Anyone who used that repair shop could damned well afford it.

There were times when something was left in a

car that would cause a great embarrassment – or worse – to the owner. Buzz cautioned him to always make the payoff a one time deal and to stick with it. Continued blackmail would lead to very serious consequences, sooner or later. That was something that was very well known for centuries. You couldn't enjoy the spoils if you were planted in a foundation pour for the new bridge or tried to swim across San Francisco Bay with two hundred pounds of log chains wrapped around you.

Evangelical preachers with TV shows were the best for that. Get some pictures or letters, even receipts from the wrong place, and they would pay big-time. They conned the ignorant and gullible out of millions a month, so what was a lousy fifty grand or so to them?

Two years, and he had more than a half mil in the bank. As soon as he could turn it into a mil, he was going to retire on a tropical island and live like a king. Beautiful women, the best food, the best clothes, the best ... everything.

Stock brokers were next. They had a habit of leaving little things in the glovecase or consol or in the space behind the seat – things like lists of the stocks they owned under another name and how they were being manipulated.

That space behind the seat was a real winner! Cash, diamond rings, lots of small items ended up there. It was a matter of knowing how to get it out without leaving traces.

He had an ability to invent things, too. He found a way to make a lean burn injection system that worked and didn't require a fancy computer to run. It was a demand/feedback system that ran on pulse feed.

He reasoned that lean burn worked when the engine was hot, which was why it wouldn't work before the engine was hot. That was simple enough!

The input had to be a thoroughly mixed, homogenized fluid. Droplets over a very small size burned unevenly, and damped.. Gases, such as butane, etc., were already in a state that was as efficient as it would get.

The lean burn had to start at normal and quickly decrease, which was why the motor raced higher and higher the last few seconds when running out of gas.

He made a system that pulsed the "run-out" in a timed cycle. It worked, gave a higher power ratio, and saved almost a quarter on gas.

Trouble was, no motor was made for that kind of variation. It would break down after a few hundred miles, at most.

He was working on a way to keep the RPMs steady, but that meant a computer, which meant nothing but problems.

He was working on that on an ancient computer in the parts storeroom that had an old Windows program that would, sometimes without any cause he could determine, put a notice on the screen, "Windows has detected a problem and will shut down in three seconds." There was nothing else except the little box you could click on that said "OK."

He giggled. He could picture a car running down the freeway at eighty when the sign came on, "AutoRun has detected a problem with the brake system and will shut down in three seconds" with only a box that said "OK,"

Three – two – one – KA-BOOM! It would, of course, have a shut-down that locked the steering, brakes, and put the transmission in Park.

He wasn't about to ever design anything that depended on computers.

He would design it to where he had it now. He could always con some millionaire into funding research. The research was already done, which would show the system was unworkable *at this time*. His out would be that it was only a matter of time, and not much of that, until the system would be workable. A little patience...?

He decided he didn't want any steady relationships. He would be perfectly happy with a lot of one-night stands. If you've got the geetus, you've got the girls. Always was true, always would be. Walk into a room wearing an Armani suit, you had a choice. Automatic! He'd proven that when he lifted a pair of Georgio Armani sunglasses from a Lexus. He went into the Double Disco wearing them. As soon as the girls saw the "Made in Italy" on one side and the "Georgio Armani" on the other, he was the center of adoring attention. The glasses, he found on the net, cost $277. Every one of those women knew the price of everything to the penny.

Personally, he preferred the three dollar pair of sunglasses he bought at a stand at the beach.

He also wore a ring (a tiny bit too large) he found in a seat. Gold with two diamonds and a large clear ruby set in a twenty two karat base. Value, according to the pawn shop, which would give a loan at ten percent, was about fourteen thousand dollars.

The women would always say something about the *beautiful* ring! He would wave it away, and say he sort of liked that one. Attractive without being ostentatious, don't you see. Very nice for casual wear.

He developed an "elite" manner of speech, with a hint of a British accent. He told them he was born in the states, but spent a good part of his youth in Merry Old, eh what? His mother was British, his father USA, but grandfather on his father's side, Scottish. Original name,

MacAndrews.

Royalty?

Oh, really, now! Titles haven't meant anything since they went on sale a few decades ago. Drove Gramps ga-ga, you see. What can you do? The old days are in the past and are going to stay there. Some holdings in several places, but it's just the business, now. What would he want with a lot of people calling him Sir Harold?

Actually, he had never been outside of California.

Actually, never outside of the Los Angeles area. He had no idea who his grandfather was on his father's side. His mother's grandmother was Dutch.

He found his "investor." Carlton Braithwaite Fishbinder, the third. Demi-royalty from somewhere like India. More money than anyone could ever use. Snobby, effete, probably gay, slightly obnoxious and condescending, suspicious to the point of paranoia, thought the whole world was conspiring to get his money.

Not in those words. Harry commiserated and said he was happy with what he had, thank you. If he was after money, a lot of people wanted to give him millions for his invention, but then they would use it to screw everyone else, and he only wanted to produce something that would make the world a little better. If he could do that one thing, his life was worthwhile. When you die, you take nothing with you and only leave a legacy. "He was rich" is not a legacy he would aspire to. A thousand of those die every day, and no one even remembers who they were in ten years.

He saw the gleam in "Carly's" eye when he said they wanted to give him millions. That would mean the invention was worth billions.

"Why not simply produce the product without them?"

"That's the trap! It would cost the million or more to get into production! I know it will make a lot, but I'm not about to produce a thing that costs a hundred dollars to make and charge two thousand for it. I don't believe in that."

"Well, I also tend to a bit of altruism, at times. Practicality makes a person do things with which he is not in total agreement, but what can you do? The world is what the world is.

"Perhaps we could make a compromise deal where both get what we want. A legacy of having done something for others, where people would say, in fifty years, that you had lived a worthwhile life."

"I don't want to talk about it. I'm sorry I even mentioned it. I know it would sell for a lot more than cost, but that would go to research on some other ideas I've had. Please! Forget I even mentioned it!"

"Oh, I'm sorry, myself. I guess I did come across as just another one who sees a lot of money from something somebody else did. I'm not that way. Honestly!"

They chatted a few minutes. Harry got a call to come in back to see what was wrong with the Rolls Royce Silver Cloud that big film star brought in. They couldn't find anything at all wrong with it.

"There's nothing wrong with it. That's the kind of thing I want to leave. A product that still performs to specs a hundred years later!"

Carly nodded and said he would talk later. He got in his Viper (that he would never drive at over sixty MPH) and left.

Harry smirked at his back.

Buzz came to say Harry was talking to Carly-Warly, and you could see the greed dripping off him. He would be the type who a hundred year old car would scream "MONEY!" to.

They did a high five.

"You can see by the readout. Fuel consumption seventy four percent. Power production one hundred forty one percent. Control factor – that's one I added – eighty three percent.

"That's my biggest sticking point. The control factor. You can see it works to prediction perfectly, but that there is still a problem.

"We can patent the process from this, but it still needs that improvement before we can put it into production.

"The reason we should get our patent now is simple enough, as I've said repeatedly: if someone else solves the control factor, it's still ours. We can make a deal for production where everyone comes out ahead."

Carl was wide-eyed at the computer readout. "I'd hoped it would save ten percent! It saves twenty six percent! It even produces more power than predicted! This is amazing!

"I think we should get the patent, but should try to solve the control thing, ourselves, but we will have that, anyhow.

"Why do you think this way is better? That somebody else can fix it? Can't you be sure we can fix it?"

"Oh, I'm sure, but it could take five years. What if somebody else has already solved it? We could be in production next week."

"Yes, yes. True. You're right. I tend to get too anxious. We'll do that. I have Fogarty, Fogarty and Goins as patent lawyers. I've used them before, but not on anything this important. We can have the patent as pending in eight months, and can go into production as soon as we have the control thing solved, which could be tomorrow!"

"I'll talk with the lawyers. We can have the pending in forty five days. It's a matter of cutting them in for one percent. I've talked with two people who have patents. They told me how to handle that!"

"You're a genius! We'll do that!

"How is funding? Within specs, like the rest of it?"

"Yes. I predicted it would cost three point four six mil. We've finished that part, and have more than half a mil to go. Everything has come out ahead of specs with this! It makes me very hopeful the rest will fall into place as fast!"

"Well, I'll ... let me make a call," Carly used his cell phone to make an appointment with the patent lawyers. They could go to the offices at four.

"They can come here at four," Harry said, sternly. "Don't let them get the upper hand or they'll manipulate you no end."

Carly was undecided. Harry took the phone and said the model and all paperwork, including the diagrams and schematics, were here. If they couldn't come, they would use another lawyer.

He listened a moment, said, "Your choice!" and started to hang up, when he was told that, Sam Goins was free, and would be there. Harry handed Carly the phone.

"You're amazing! I wish I had the balls to talk to them like that!"

"They'll have to respect us. Don't ever let any lawyer get the upper hand.

"I'm going to take a vacation while we wait for the patent. I'm tired and irritable. I've not gotten much sleep lately. I need to relax before I go into the intense research about the control factor."

"Yes, yes! Of course! I know you've been working tirelessly for weeks! You deserve a respite!"

Actually, he had all the stuff except the computer link done before he even met Carly. He had installed the injectors and ran a computer analysis the past four days. Three hours per day. The hard part was to run the engine at a RPM setting that wouldn't blow it apart for the analysis. The analysis was a comparison with the engine before the injection system was installed. The control factor was a change in wording from "Degree of engine stress" and was read in inverse ratio. In reality, what it said was that the engine was stressed eighty five percent more. It didn't say that was at minimum RPMs.

They went to lunch at a fine restaurant, Carly's treat (like the two mil Harry had in his account wasn't Carly's treat).

At a quarter to four they were back at the little garage they rented to meet with Goins. Goins watched the running test and was amazed at the comparison, which Harry had on video to show that it was an honest test.

"Well, I can predict that this will make on the order of four billion dollars in five years, then will get steadily better!" Goins decreed. "I have experience with this sort of thing, and a product that performed about ten percent as well has made nearly a billion in three years."

They signed all the papers (Goins had a secretary along to watch the process and notarize everything) and made copies to use in the patenting process. Harry explained that they would need to solve one more thing before they went into production. Carly said it was really minor, and didn't infringe on the patent. It was merely a safety factor. You know how the government is on that, nowadays. Extreme. Probably no problem as it sat, but might as well be sure before they got into a lot of silly red tape, ha, ha, ha.

They were soon gone. Harry took the injection system off the engine and replaced the original. Carly asked why.

"We are applying for a patent. That is public information. Leave something like this around and someone else is going to apply for a patent that conflicts, we end up in court spending fifty million to fight them – or let them give us ten million to drop out."

"Who would do such a thing?!"

"Name any big oil company. Get an education of the history of this kind of thing. If they can get a patent, they quash it. I know of a couple of things they did exactly that with."

"Well, I have heard stories."

"It ain't gonna happen here! It's not about the ten million or so they would pay us, and not about the billions we could get with it, it's about stopping them from screwing everyone in the world another time."

"Yes. Their sales would naturally falter from the efficiency of our invention. Twenty five percent loss? That would amount to billions a year! Trillions!"

"So. You *do* get it!

"I think I'll take a Caribbean cruise. I always wanted to!"

"You've certainly earned that!"

Harry leaned on the rail and smiled at Jeannie. She was today's little side piece. Beautiful, sexy, fun, dumb as dirt. Just his type!

"Well, I didn't like Haiti. At all!" Jeannie said, pouting. "All those dirty little kids begging, and the attitude of the blacks, just because we're white! I mean, I didn't do anything to their grandma!"

"Yes. The culture thrives on blaming somebody else for what their great grandfather endured in another place at another time with another cast of characters. It's the stylish thing to do, it seems. We're so repressed!"

"Yeah, sure. And the president of the US is black. How repressed can you get? They act like that, and blame it on us."

"Haiti is poor. I can understand a certain resentment, but it's the ones in the states who keep it going. Lack of responsibility for yourself.

"I think I'll go to my cabin and relax for a couple hours while it's so hot out here."

"Want company?"

"Why not?"

Two hours later he was at the top deck pool. He took care of himself, so was a lot of competition for the fat soft types and the gigolos. The gigolos could have those flabby older women. He was the one who was more than presentable and who could buy the ship if he wanted.

Well, not quite. Good thing he didn't want any ship.

Gloria, a rather hot, fiery Latina, came to stand beside him. He ordered a Daquiri for her and said he spoke with her last evening at the dance floor. Was the man she was with her husband or just a boyfriend?

"Oh, just a man I met at dinner. We shared a table, and we went to the dance together from there. I'm not married and don't have a steady. I'm on the cruise to have a little fun. I have to get back to work next week. I'm a sales representative for an automobile company – which means I dress like this and give every man who walks by a sexy look and hand them a flyer.

"What the hell. It pays. Very well.

"You married? Or gay? Anyone I've met I could like was one or the other."

"Not married and only gay on alternate Thursdays, when I can find which Thursday I want to start. Never seemed the right time yet."

She laughed. "Maybe we can get together tonight. We can discuss the movements of heavenly bodies. Ours."

"Sounds like a plan!"

In the morning they were just coming into Puerto Rico. Annette, a girl he met at breakfast, said she hoped it was better than Haiti. Was he going on to Barbados?

"Yes. I might stay there for a few days. I know too many from Jamaica back home, so don't think I'd like it.

"Of course, the people there might not be so many drug dealers and thugs, but the impression from home tells me I would *not* like Jamaica."

"I think I might. I'm a woman, and they treat us better than some – but there are too many anywhere who think they want to act like those rappers. I have pepper spray and know a few moves."

They talked a bit, then went aground together. Puerto Rico was alright, some great and some not so great. They would stay in port for the night, so he and Annette made the rounds.

In the morning Annette left his cabin and he straightened out his stuff and sent some things to the laundry. He was ready for Barbados, so went to the upper deck to mingle. A very handsome jock type came to where he was sitting in the shade of an umbrella by the pool and asked if he wanted company. He waved to the seat on the other side of the little table.

He introduced himself as Louis Franks, from Chicago. He was on the cruise because he won a raffle. He was bored.

"I'd think you would have plenty of company. You're the type all those women want to lay on this kind of cruise."

"I get lots of offers. Some want to pay me. I don't want women."

"Oh."

"I'm not trying to pick you up. You wouldn't. I'm not interested in any of the hustlers. I don't care how big a dong some guy has. If I can't respect him, I don't want him. I can't respect a whore, male or female.

"Well, it depends on circumstances. I can't respect any of the type who come on these cruises.

"I just need someone to pal around with. I won't interfere with your action. I can tell you aren't a hustler. You already have a lot more than any ten on this ship. I've noticed you and the women. Another one every couple of hours. I have a cabin three from yours. More power to you, but you can use some rest, I would think."

They chatted for awhile. Harry didn't have a lot of contacts with the gay lifestyle. He had been a bit repulsed by it, but kept an open mind. Lou was a lot of fun and had a great sense of humor. There would never be more than friendship between them, but Harry did consider him a friend after the afternoon. They went to dinner together. Harry left with Ginger after dinner.

Lou said he was a sex addict. Maybe he was. Great life!

In the morning they came into Barbados. Harry liked the looks of the island. He liked the happy people and the laidback lifestyle. As he was going aground, Lou came to ask if he wanted company. Say so if the answer was "No."

They went aground, laughing at a joke Lou told about a priest and a rabbi meeting an evangelical missionary on Barbados.

They found a hotel where Harry left his stuff, then went around the area. Lou met a man who he seemed to click with. Harry wished him luck and went around the area a bit. He really did like the place and the lifestyle. He seemed to fit.

He met Irena, a really pretty woman with a great personality. She seemed interested in him, not so much his money.

He stayed in Barbados three days and nights. With Irena.

He then hired a boat to show him around the neighboring islands, then to go more south and closer to Central America.

He found the place. It was a small island with a house and dock. There were about twenty natives on the island, but they did not own it. They would leave if Harry bought it and wanted them to.

"No. I'll buy it if the price is right. You stay. It's your home."

"You are a good man. Enrique, who owns it now, is a good man, but we have to work for him to stay."

"You can work for whoever you like. The island

is about six hectares. I see that you all live on the south two hectares. I'll deed that to you. I want friends around, not employees."

He wasn't from a hugging society. He found it was really pleasant for these people to hug him.

Well, it cost him a million one fifty. He still had a million. He would make a deal and move here. It had everything he could want in a place. Anything else, he could import.

Harry went into the garage where the motor was sitting on its stand. Sure enough, the place had been broken into several times. He smirked at Carly.

"So. Nothing new. I said they would try that, but they didn't get anything. That leaves it to where we'll get offers for millions for the patent rights. We should get the pending in a few days, at most. It'll then be up to them to make offers.

"Carly, I've done some intense study while I was on the ship. I am in a bad state here, because, to make it work, we need materials that simply do not exist now. What they have is for the space program and costs fifty times what we could put in engines that would stand the stress. In short, we produce more power from less fuel than anything we have will stand. It will blow the motor apart.

"It's like that trillion dollar plane the military built. It doesn't work, and can't.

"You have about four million in it, and I have all my work for years. I say we sell to the highest bidder. You can make a big profit, and we can drive it as high as it will go. It's better to get ten or twelve million now than to wait ten years and maybe still get nothing."

"Well, ten million for four isn't a bad investment. Less than a year. If we have to, we have to. Maybe it will also make a big drain on the oil companies, millions more for research that will end them up where they started.

"I'll agree to that."

"It's a matter of waiting for them to contact us, so we'll have to act like we want to start production as soon as we have the pending. We'll start asking questions about a plant and warehouse, and about distribution methods."

"I see. If they think we have the problem solved, they will be desperate to stop its production."

"We know at least four of them tried to steal it, so maybe they'll compete."

"Let's hope!"

Three days later the pending came through. Carly and Harry had asked questions of realtors and distribution centers and for specs for injectors from all the car manufacturers. Harry spotted the two who were watching the garage where they had made the tests.

Harry got a call. From a large oil company. From the acquisitions department head, a Mrs. Livingston. She wished an appointment to discuss the new innovation in fuel economy. Perhaps they could make it easier to install the manufacturing process, and they would have to know if the process used a special fuel.

Harry said he didn't have the time today, or possibly this week. His days were pretty well booked up.

She suggested they meet at a very famous restaurant, her treat. She wished to get in on the ground floor on such an important process.

Harry said that he and his partner would be there. He would have a date, that was already promised. He didn't know if Carly would have a date. He hoped his date wouldn't be put off because of mixing business and pleasure, but she had to understand how a new business made huge demands on time.

He hung up. "Do you really have a date for tonight?" Carly asked.

"I will. Maybe that Susan who we met at the distribution center? She'll get a kick out of it. I liked her sense of fun."

He called her. She said it really would be fun. She always wanted to eat at the Imperial, but never had enough money. Two day's salary for the aperitif? Seven thirty would be fine.

They went into the restaurant on the dot. Carly said he would consider Mrs. Livingston his date, if she looked like the picture in Executives of Note. She was recently divorced, so there were possibilities. She made one twenty thou a year plus bonuses, which amounted to over half a million last year.

She looked like the picture, but a bit older. She was still an attractive woman in her early thirties. Carly was forty two, so found himself interested.

The dinner was superb. Susan was a lot of fun. She got along with everyone. Anna Livingston loosened up and got along well with Carly. She had checked on him before any of this, so knew he was worth some hundreds of millions. She was like him. The bottom line. She had "independent means" and he was richer than Midas. Harry remarked to Susan, when Carly and Anna were on the dance floor, that he saw a budding romance.

"To tell the truth, which I do sometimes, they deserve each other. I don't suppose she's quite as bad as she seemed at first, and neither is he."

"When I first met him I thought he was just another greedbag who was after the money. He's a greedbag, but has a good feature here and there. He's not so bad."

"How much will you get from this?"

"We're shooting for about ten mil. We could get it into the hundred mil range, but I don't want that anymore, and Carly will come out ahead. It's just a game to him."

They went home about three hours later. Their first offer was five million, which Harry put on an act about how their preliminary research cost them nearly that, and it was his major work for more than six years. They didn't want to put a lot more into it, but it would cost five or six mil more to get into full production. Luckily, most parts could be ordered from the shelf. There were only two that would have to be made. Pre-orders expected to be nearly a billion, so thanks, but no thanks.

He had an e-mail message from another company when he got home that Susan got a kick out of. *Don't make any deals with anyone about your invention until we talk. It is worth a lot more than they will offer, and they won't include future royalties. We will.*

Harry dropped the computer from online and they went to bed.

In the morning there were two people who came to his door before eight o'clock. He said they could go to the shop later. He would be there, as would Carly. They worked everything as a team.

When he picked up Carly at that ridiculous mansion he inhabited, Carly said people were driving him crazy. There had to be twenty who wanted to speak with him on matters of the most serious gravity. Harry told about the ones he got. They had already agreed to tell all of them to meet them at the shop after nine.

They went to breakfast. Harry dropped Susan off at her apartment and he and Carly went to a local diner for coffee and to waste time. They managed to get to the shop at ten after nine. There were at least a dozen people wandering around on the sidewalk. They invited the bunch inside. It was obvious that some of the people definitely did *not* like others. Three of them almost got into a fist fight right there. Harry told them they could act like they weren't raised in a pigstye or they could leave.

The bidding started. It got to eighty million before Harry put up his hands and said they didn't want any eighty million dollars. They wanted a deal where this wasn't used to screw everyone. Carly was in back, so they couldn't see him when he staggered and looked like he would faint.

"Write an offer, and include what will be done with cash monies over the amount wanted. What that is will determine who gets the patent rights. If you can't think beyond money, don't bother to offer anything. I am not money oriented. I want enough to live the life I want, which includes people I think are worth the time and effort.

"That can be a hint about what to include.

"I will be in touch. Don't call me. I'll call you.

"I have an appointment. You can drop your proposition in this box. Everything here is recorded, so trying to remove anything will be noted.

"Have a nice day. The last one to leave, please turn out the lights and release the catch on the door lock."

He walked out with Carly, who was just getting his legs back.

When they were in the car, Carly whined, "What did you mean! We could get a hundred million easily!"

"What would you do with it?"

"It would be security. I could make some major investments!"

"That would make you even more money that you could invest to make even more. Can't you see how pointless that is?"

"I know your argument, and agree, intellectually. I can't stop myself when it comes to money. There's never enough."

"The money owns you. You don't own it. Over a certain amount is useless. I meant it about legacy. I'll want anything those greedbags offer to be used for the Harold Anderson Fund. That will be my legacy. If I ever have a family, I want to leave them the island I bought and enough to get by. They have to learn to earn what they get. I learned that the hard way.

"You know how I got enough to start this with you?"

"I suppose friends helped finance it."

"No. I stole it. I don't want my kids in that kind of position. I want them to have enough to live, if they choose not to aim higher. I want them to have the drive to go after the higher goal. I aimed at pie in the sky – and got it. I want them to have that drive, but not to have to do what I did to get there. I want my name known and respected a hundred years after I'm ashes spread on the sea."

"I think, just maybe, that'll happen. You have a certain window in time to accomplish that, then time's up.

"What do you think will happen – and can I get ten million out of it? Just to keep the score card high."

"We'll learn exactly where the bullshit is and where anyone actually feels anything in that crowd. You can get ten. I want about four more, so I'll take five in case of emergency."

"Sounds like a plan!"

"You and Anna get along, huh?"

"Yes. It surprised me. She likes money for different reasons than do I. She is interested in dating more. I asked if that held in the case her company didn't get the deal. She said she wouldn't even try anymore. That's why she wasn't at the meeting.

"She wants to get away from that company. She doesn't like how they do business and she doesn't like the ones she has to do business with.. She likes me because I'm not that kind."

"You're not that kind to extremes."

"You have a point."

"I wish you well."

"And I, you. I started out thinking I would use some yokel who didn't have a clue as to what he had. I was going to get billions and you would get a couple of million and think you's made a great deal."

Harry laughed. "I was going to clean this greedbag out and let him learn how it was to live like I always had to."

They both got a good laugh at that. Carly wiped his eyes and said, "Aren't you glad we were both wrong?"

"Know something? Yeah!"

"Well, let's see what's in the box. I had to turn off the phone and have the police stop people from coming onto the property. Now, it's preachers and such who have projects they just know I will agree with, mainly to save the souls of wayward children of god and to buy a new yacht or plane to use in spreading god's almighty word."

"To which you answered?" Carly asked.

"I'm an atheist, and if there is a god, he would certainly not need such as them to tell me about him."

"I would argue, but know you can shoot me down. I guess I'm more agnostic. I believe, more and more, that it's all bullshit. I've gone on the net to Facebook and YouTube and such and lurked on the groups. It's true that the religious sites don't permit argument. Argue and you're suddenly not there anymore. The creationist versus evolutionists have yet to produce one item of proof, while the evolutionists have mountains of proof.

"I compartmentalize that kind of thing.

"What do we have?"

"Hmm. 'We propose to offer you one hundred million dollars, flat, with no strings attached, and you will receive royalties of three percent for perpetuity.' No column.

"Next, 'We offer eighty five million dollars cash, which you will dictate as to disbursement.' Another one that's all about money. They do say we can do what we want with the money, but that's true of any of it.

"This is rich! 'We offer one hundred million in cash for full rights. I do not understand what you mean about the rest of it.' We're getting on a linear response on just the third one!

"How about, 'We offer fifty million cash, royalties in perpetuity, and fifty million to be disbursed as to your instructions.' A tiny bit closer.

"This is sort of an expected response. 'Meet with me. I will better any other offer by ten percent.' We can have some fun with those.

"Now, 'We will disburse one hundred million dollars as to your instructions, for which we will receive all rights.' Not even close, in one way.

"This may be one to consider. 'We will offer ninety million dollars to be used per your instructions. You will receive three percent royalties on any sales for perpetuity. We will guarantee to continue research on this process, in case there are problems. We can see that there may be a stress problem, but are confident we can overcome this obstacle.' First one in the possibility pile."

They were all so close to the same it was boring. Two had suggested that they would better any offer by ten percent.

"Carly! Call Anna. Tell her we will agree that the deal is false in a separate legal contract! Tell her to offer us, say, four hundred million, three hundred thousand plus continuing royalties of five percent!"

"Why? That seems ... so we can see how high those two 'better offer' idiots will go?"

"Uh-huh."

"I think she'll go along. She doesn't like those people at all." He made the call. She said she would make a proposal that could be proven false later because it would be obvious that E. E. F. Longshire's signature is a forgery. She wanted to be in on the meeting with those two so she could sit back and look smug and superior.

They waited, then went to Anna's office. She handed them a very legal-looking contract proposal on company letterhead. Carly called the two, saying he had to argue with Harry about their proposal, because the one they had was better than they ever expected. They would meet at the local McDonald's to discuss it. One hour.

They made jokes and madeup scenarios about how this would go down.

"Well, Mr. Betts, was it? And Ms. Watson? You both know why we're here. Harry has argued against even bothering, but I am more prone to seeking the best deal, as you undoubtably have learned. If you haven't learned that, you are not fit for you job description.

"Do you known Mrs. Livingston? It is her company who has made the top offer. Here are copes of the offer. You may wish to consult with superiors before you act on your notes at this morning's meeting." He handed them the copies.

Watson actually fell off her chair. Betts turned sickly white and began to sweat. "Four hundred million?" He squeaked.

"Yes," Anna replied. "We did a survey and find that the product in subject here will return three billion dollars in three years, so it is a good investment. We will finish the small necessary research and will market the product ourselves, considering that it will reduce the supply end's profits less than that, it is a strong investment for that reason. Mr. Andrews has another idea, based on the discoveries of Nikola Tesla, that could well make oil dependence a dinosaur, in toto. You will note that the contract guarantees us first rights to that process, which will be dependant on factors at the time.

"We in the oil business are on the way out. I-Oil intends to not let that be a disaster to our investments."

Harry and Carly were in back where they couldn't be heard. Harry asked, "Where did she get the Tesla bit?"

"She saw it on the web. Someone has developed a motor that will work in space by some kind of microwave thing, where microwaves are already there in a lot more quantity than the process uses.

"I have no idea what that's about, but she said there was an article about the fact we're constantly bombarded with microwaves right here. If they're harnessed, we have the free energy in any quantity for the taking.

"She's a brilliant woman."

"Do you wish to better our offer?" Anna asked, smirking. Betts had to make a call. Watson said she hasn't the authority to go over two hundred fifty million. She left.

Betts came back in and said they would go to half a billion, but would retain all rights. Period. That included the future projects clause.

"Add ten percent," Anna said, quickly.

Betts almost charged her. She smirked. Betts stormed out.

"Care for a good dinner? My treat?" Carly suggested.

"Okay, but not here," Anna fired back. They giggled.

They went to a close restaurant that had very

good food that was prepared well. Harry left shortly after the meal and went to his apartment to clean up. Maybe he would go to that new dance/ live entertainment bar to see who would be around who might ... no. He was actually too tired for that tonight. It wouldn't kill him to not have a woman for one lousy night.

He hoped.

"Well, it's time to start the rest of my life," Harry said to Carly as they finished the wording to the agreement for the invention. Mega-Oil had somehow gotten a copy of the "Anna Paper" as they called it, had seen the logic to it, and would finish the research along the lines in that contract. It did not include rights to future projects, but gave Harry ten million and Carly ten million, then would open the Andrews-Fishbinder Fund at 80 million, which would educate promising poor students, fund research into natural cures and anything else that would raise the standard of living for the poorer people, among other things.

Carly announced that he and Anna were getting married, both as a business deal and because they really did get along well and cared about each other.

The first project of the A-F Fund was to purchase a large plot in Panamá where *Artemisia annua* would be raised for free treatment of

Leishmaniasis and other parasites and as a cancer cure to be distributed, along with methods of preparation and living plants to be raised in all the indigenous populations in Central and South America. It also was useful against malaria. Millions of people would benefit. There would be continuing research in a facility there concerning natural plant remedies.

Harry then moved to his island. He would stay there seven years, then would find another project. That Tesla process had him intrigued.

The trip to the island was much like the first, just the names were different. He met Louis, who had fallen in love with Barbados and decided to stay for awhile. They had a good time, then Harry picked up his boat and headed for his paradise. He had seven years, if he didn't get bored or something, to explore the area and the people. He would learn all he could. It was his nature. He would use the internet to keep up with the rest of the world and to research whatever caught his interest.

He had to buy a satellite connection, but it was only twelve hundred dollars, and connected him to the world.

"Only twelve hundred dollars." A short time ago, that would have been beyond his ability to even consider.

Yes, life could be good. It could be better than

good. He had all this on what was first to be a scam, then turned into something else. His desire for money turned from all in the world to what he needed to be comfortable and live the way he wanted, no apologies. He had his legacy.

Time would tell if he had direct heirs to be proud of his legacy.

He didn't bring a woman. He liked the people on the island, and two were, so far as he knew, single and attractive. There were a number of islands within two hours in his boat. He was sure there were plenty of women there. Two were tourist stops, so that was a definite.

The old tune from South Pacific came to mind as he docked. Bali Hi, may call you ....

Well, he'd answered the call, and was not disappointed.

<u>*Decision*</u>

Harry Andrews finally got the perfect scam done! He was living his dream life! He knew there was a time limit on the dream. It was now. Was he ready to go forward, or would he stagnate right there?

He sighed and rolled over to stare out the window to the beach. It was a glorious sunrise. He was looking directly east out of that window. Maria smiled and said breakfast was ready. This morning would be melon, hojaldres, bolitas, coffee, and guanabana chicha.

Maria was the niece of one of the people on his island. She had come to visit two years ago. It was an immediate mutual attraction. She was intelligent and very pretty, not the bimbo sexpot type. She didn't put up with BS and neither did he. The long shiny black hair was a major turn-on.

"You got today marked on the calendar. What's that?"

"Time's up. I have to start a new life today – or not. I think I'm ready for something to do other than check up on my projects once a month. It's seven years today, and I'm ready to move on.

"I think I'll work on the microwave thing. It's

sort of intriguing, in its own way. There was a thing or two on the net. I kept up with it."

"Yah. You gonna be here, or do I find me another man?"

It was a joke between them. He might get tired of her and find another woman, she might get tired of him and find herself another man.

"I'll be here as much as usual. I'll get what equipment I need and build a little lab in back"

"Damn!"

He slapped her on the butt and they both laughed.

He got up, had the delicious breakfast, and strolled on the beach for an hour or so, then returned to gather a few clothes and such. He took his debit card in its case and his passport, then said he was off to Barbados, probably to the states, then would be back with a load of crap he would need. It wouldn't be a lot, probably. Quite a few of the things were already researched to the point he wouldn't have to bother with them.

He checked his notes one more time and printed out a list of things he would need.

He's read a book called The Zero Theory, which seemed a pointless rambling until certain point were considered, then $0/0 = 1$, another book by the same author. None of it seemed connected, at first, then he related what was said to Einstein, which made a couple of points clearer, then had studied Nikola Tesla, and saw a very strong connection.

It could very well be true that there was unlimited energy, ready for he taking, all around us at all times. It was a matter of learning how to use it.

He had read a few things by the same author where an electronic sling was used. It seemed a SciFi invention, at the time, but combining the ideas suggested it could work.

Hah! Here was an uneducated slob who was working with Einsteinian concepts and Tesla's ideas and some nutcase author's inventions!

He made what he thought the electronic sling would be. It worked, to a limited extent. It was based more on $0/0 = 1$ than the others. Time and motion were all that existed. $TM = 1$. Increase T and you automatically reduce M. As the books stated, the equation remains in balance at all times. Motion = Velocity. All the world was using their efforts to increase velocity, which was why all the energy was needed. Would it be easier and more efficient to simply decrease time?

It was an intriguing if silly proposition, in one way. It could use some consideration, in another.

Why think about that now?

Why not? He was looking for a project.

He kissed Maria goodbye and left the dock, thinking about the equation.

It fell into place. He could make the sling, and it would work.

That was a project he was not going to pursue. An indefensible weapon that any ten year old kid with normal intelligence could throw together with things found around the house? A weapon that could bring down the Stealth Bomber and anything less? A weapon any terrorist in the word could build in a couple of hours?

Civilization would collapse. Millions, even billions, would be doomed. Human nature would turn it into a conflict that wouldn't be completely resolved as long as two people existed.

Increase motion and reduce time. That was all it was about. Basically, Einsteinian time dilation put into effect. In crease motion and decrease time. Point A to point B. Reduce the time it took to move between the points – and inertia increased in direct ratio. A 10 gram object that, in effect, was traveling at 30K MPS, would go through the best armor ever produced!

Okay. Forget that.

By the time he reached the dock in Barbados he was back to the free energy part. While the sling was all bad news, the energy could be good news.

He checked with suppliers in Barbados. It was as he feared. He had to go to the states to get what he needed.

He sighed deeply and headed for the airport. He

stored his boat at the dock in drydock lockup.

He landed in Houston (Hell concentrated), where he immediately went to a hotel in a cheaper section. He didn't care to be recognized.

Not gonna happen, Charlie! There was a watch on his passport. The minute he got the stamp in Barbados it was noted. He got a call less than half an hour after booking in. FBI.

FBI? Oh, shit! Those big companies were worried that he was going to make a big stink about his invention never being made available, and it was common knowledge everywhere except the states that the government was owned totally by big corporations.

He said that he was there to visit old friends, buy a few things for his newer research, and leave. He didn't give a shit about the invention. He doubted they had made it work yet. His research on the net would tell him if they had developed a way to use it without super-expensive alloys.

No, he had no intention of contacting anyone in the big companies at this time.

He noted that he was followed everywhere. He found a place where he could get certain chemicals. The big thing was platinum in a usable form, which he solved by getting a hundred pound sack of pellets used in exhaust converters. Phosphorus was no problem. It was a matter of absorption, not deflecting, and transforming energy forms. Tesla's tower had some answers, but not in areas anyone would consider.

He took two days to find all of what he might need. He was ready to get the hell out of the states.

At the airport he was denied passage. His baggage was suspect and there was a hold on his passport. He was need for testimony about the death of Carlton Fishbinder.

Carly? He'd e-mailed him two days ago to say he would probably be in the states! He was dead?

Harry called Anna. She said he had an accident in his helicopter. It lost power somehow and crashed in San Francisco Bay! She didn't believe it for one second! That chopper was in better condition than any other in the world. Carly saw to it!

What was going on?

He told her to take very careful steps to secure her safety. He was going through an unbelievable set of stalls, himself. Carly may be dead because Harry came to the states, which made some big corporations very nervous.

His early life in Los Angeles gave him a good knowledge of how to get out and to his island. He would stay among as many people as possible.

He sent all the things he'd collected to Barbados as deck freight, then went to the FBI offices. He went in the front and to the reception desk, asked for a couple of forms, and went to sit by the elevator to seem to be filling out forms. When he saw his follower getting on an elevator, he casually walked out, went through his pockets to find how they could trace him. He took out his debit card and slipped it into a metal case. And his passport. That was probably how they were tracing him. The chip.

He hooked the case to a cell phone battery and slipped into a little café to order a couple of tacos and coffee. After a few minutes he went to the restroom, made a few quick changes – such as cutting about six inches off his hair and making a mustache and beard with the hair. He shaved deep widow's peaks on his scalp and wrapped just enough paper toweling around his mid-section to make him look pudgy. He changed his shirt for one he'd bought earlier in a second-hand store and ditched the fancy shoes for Crocs. He put a pebble in the left Crock that hurt just a bit when he stepped on it, so he tended to have a very slight hitch in his walk.

He was expert at this. It wasn't a busy time of morning, so he had the time. He walked out looking a lot different than when he walked in.

Now to the Mexican section. His Spanish was very good. He used it with Maria all the time.

He found a man by using the code name they used in LA.

He was in Mexico three hours later as Samuél Garcia G. In Mexico City six hour later as Fredrico Binz L. He got his passport "stamped" for Barbados, then went to the airport, where he caught a flight as himself, minus the disguise.

He would have no more than half an hour after Barbados before they traced him. He called to have Louis get his boat out of drydock and have it ready to go as soon as the plane landed..

He was on his island just after dark. He was going to make a sling. He had a project. He was going to break all those big oil companies. Carly was going a long way too far to ignore or excuse.

Lou brought his boat to the dock. Ernesto, a good friend who lived on the island, went to collect the things Lou had brought from the cargo carrier boat. A boat was sitting not far out in the Caribbean. It came by the island regularly. It had come ashore on the far side once at night and two men came ashore and looked around a bit. They were going to set up a little transmitter in a bunch of mangroves.

The transmitter suddenly had a hole in it, as did two of the three engines on their boat.

They got the message. It is a lot easier to shoot a hole in a person than in an outboard motor.

Harry had made a small sling.

Harry went into intense study and research. He

had fifty or more things that wouldn't work – and, finally, one that did.

He took a sheet of aluminum foil, put a plug connector to it, coated it with a layer of a chemicals and then another. He plugged the meter to it and watched. Fourteen point thee one volts at point two four amps. From a piece four inches by four inches.

The next was 10" X 10" and gave a reading of fourteen point three one volts at one point six amps.

He put it outside in the sunlight. Same reading. Inside in a closet. Same reading. In the daytime, same reading. At night, same reading.

He had his free energy.

He made a panel a meter by a meter. 33.84 amps. That would run the house, nicely. It would run his boat with an electric motor. A converter was all he needed.

He estimated it cost $67.75 to make the meter square panel. It would last at least ten years, if not a lot longer.

He had to have a solid patent. It wouldn't be possible to hide the application. He would be dead in minutes.

If it was for that device, that panel.

But, could he ... he had it! He called Goins, the patent attorney.

"I was working on an energy collector system

that could give enough power to run a house for low cost. I have a process that will power a calculator, maybe a cell phone or such. It will supply free energy at that level for more than five years.

"It isn't what I was looking for. Not cell phones, but it should make a bundle that would finance more research. It gives me something to do.

"I want to get a patent, but, well, I may be able to expand it a bit and get more power, but it seems to give me fourteen volts. Period.

"Does the patent have to be for one size, or is it for the process, not the size?"

"For the basic idea. Size doesn't matter. You have to include the variations in the patent or someone else can change one, say, diode and claim it's different."

"Well, I will be first, so can make enough to keep on. Do you need the same things as with the injectors?"

"Basically. A working model and all schematics or whatever."

"Well, the thing is only four inches by four inches and I have all the schematics and whatevers. I can't come there. As you probably know, Carly was murdered because I went to visit some people and buy some supplies. They tried to keep me there. They're watching the island."

"I'll send a woman for the stuff. You know what

I need, so can have it ready. I can handle all of it from here."

"I'll get it all together and will have it in Barbados. When she gets there, have her call me. I'll have it set up to get the stuff to her. They will, of course, intercept the call and be there pretty fast, so it has to be fast."

"Yeah. Same thing with the industrial spies. I can handle that."

They talked a bit more about Carly. That was to let the FBI or CIA or whatever know he had a way to get information out that they couldn't stop, short of closing down the net – which would put them out of business. Harry knew the throwaway phone he was using would take them a few minutes to trace, so had gotten his message across before they could find his signal. He used the extra time to tell Goins he had built a sling, and had used it against his surveillors. It was already described on more than fifty websites in thirty countries, was something anyone could make in a couple of hours, and could shoot down any plane or hole and motor or pump, even heavily armored stuff. It would not get distributed if he sent a code at certain pre-set times.

"Shoot down any plane?" Goins asked. "That would stop ... really?"

"They can check the holes in their outboards with a scientist and get confirmation on that. If anything happens to me beyond getting slightly pissed, it's the end of civilization as we know it."

"It is? How?"

"Shoot down any plane? Hole any motor, tank, pump, generator, what have you from a distance of as much as ten kilometers? No food or fuel or water delivery, no transportation, no electricity? Almost any ten year old kid can make the thing.

"I suppose Israel will be first to be eliminated, then the big corporation CEOs and major stockholders. I doubt there would be a politician left alive anywhere in the world in a day. Literally hundreds of millions of people starving.

"Once I get this energy thing done and can get on with my research I might take all that off, but it stays there until we have some kind of agreement with guarantees. I won't fall for a BS line. Not after Carly."

"Well, I'll look into your suggestions. Maybe we can get a process started. Tesla may have already patented something they could use to claim infringement. I understand your predicament."

"Thanks. I'll be in touch."

Seeing he had sent what the patent process needed with Lou, this might work out. He had to stay alive a few more months, then could control things very well.

It was the next day when he got the call that the representative of the patent lawyer was in

Barbados. He knew how to get the model and schematics to her before the CIA or whoever could react. They were watching him, not her.

He called Lou. "Plan A. At position A. Fast!"

"I'm half a minute away. Done!"

Ten minutes later Lou called and said that "George and Bill" were going to catch the cruise ship that was just pulling out from the wharf and would deliver the papers to Vincente in Cancún the following afternoon.

That meant the model and papers were delivered to the woman, who would be on the private small plane leaving in twelve minutes. She would get a commercial flight from Kingston as soon as they could arrive.

Tomorrow would tell if the plan worked. Harry and Maria walked along the beach. He waved at the boat sitting about a kilometer offshore. He could pretty well know they were watching him.

<u>*The Waiting Game*</u>

Maria came to knock on the lab door and say there was a man from California there to see him. He seemed a nervous type. Should she have the people throw him off the island or would Harry talk to him?

He said to take their guest to the porch facing the sea and bring him whatever he wanted to drink. He would finish what he was working on in about ten minutes.

It was 47 days since the patent application. It should be a legal pending phase by now. It was being held up, but there could be a very quick solution to that. He could threaten to go public about the injector invention, which would put the big corporations in a bad spot, seeing as there were all those lawsuits about fracking and such.

He finished what he was working on (nothing) and went to the porch twenty five minutes later to find a stiff-looking executive type sitting there, staring at the sea.

"Very tranquil. I'm Harry, as you probably know."

"Evander Hallworthy. Hell of a name to be stuck with. Friends call me Vandy."

"What do you want, Mr. Hallworthy?"

"I get the point. I'm representing an international group of businessmen. We have to know something about a ... we know about the weapon, of course. You knew that. We have to know something about it, and if it's real."

"You didn't have scientific tests made on those outboards?"

"Yes, we did. That is why the concern. Part of what you've claimed appears to be true."

"I haven't claimed anything, and the only way you could know what I've *described* about it would be through illegal surveillance. Everything I said is fact. I would think, by now, you would know I don't deal in, shall we say, disinformation and subterfuge."

"Could you demonstrate it for me?"

"No. It's too easy to see what it is and how it's made. If it gets out, you won't need my releasing of it. It will be out, and anyone, including the nearest ten year old, can figure on how to make it. The ones you would have constructing it would be like you, and would figure on an angle where they were top dog, so they would make one for themselves – but one may not be enough, so make several and distribute them to your own little group, each of whom would figure they could be the top dog, and it's all over for the whole damned crooked greedy world.."

"I will swear to not let..."

"What part of 'no' don't you understand?"

"I see."

"What does holding up my patent for a toy, in effect, accomplish?"

"Beg pardon?"

"I invented a sort of battery thing to use in charging cell phones and calculators and such. It should be through by now. It's not. DUH! It's to finance another project."

"I know nothing about it. I will check. A moment?" He took out a strange-looking cell phone and spoke, without punching a key. "Information. Now! What about a patent applied for by Andrews that is being held up?"

There was a pause of about ten seconds and an answer Harry couldn't hear.

"Are they really that stupid? It doesn't occur to them that he isn't interested in toys, so wouldn't invent something like that he would patent? Don't any of them have the intelligence to see it was a test to see if they would do that? Do they have a clue as to the fact they have given themselves away to the very last person on Earth they wanted to ... my God! A simple, obvious trap, and they fell into it? Am I totally surrounded by incompetents? Christ almighty! How damned *stupid* are they?"

He dropped the phone in his pocket and shook

his head. "What now?"

"Can't you see all I want is to be left alone? Didn't the patent thing even tell you that? Why else make the test?"

"Except to expose exactly what it exposed. We can't ... Mr. Andrews, we have to know how to defense ourselves against your weapon!"

"I'm very fortunate there. There is no defense. If there were, you would already have found it and you wouldn't be here and I would be dead.."

Maria called from inside, "Hare! Goins said to tell you he just got a call, some guy in a panic, and the patent pending official declaration will be in his hands within the hour!"

Harry giggled. Hallworthy raised an eyebrow.

"I figured that you would see the patent as a test. (He hadn't. It was a surprise that Hallworthy came up with that.) It was a game of plus/minus. If you thought that I thought that you thought that I thought, you would act the way I thought you thought if I stopped at the right one. Fifty-fifty. I did."

"Which means the patent is important? It was a real application for a real thing?"

"Uh-huh. Sell your oil stocks – or have the sense to do what Anna's people will do."

"Which is?"

"Get in on the production end of this. It's still about energy, just not the same one. The oil bit will phase way down. You will still need lubricants and such, road surfacing, jet fuel – for transportation, not military bullshit. A hell of a lot of products that don't pollute. You can capitalize on that. All of a sudden, oil companies are leading the environmental concern people. If you could see through your personal greeds you could come out way ahead on this kind of thing. So could the world."

"I don't like reformers, but it's something like that or disaster, isn't it?"

"Yep! Your choice. You are right here at the inception, so can be a leader. Remember that you are being listened to right now, so some others are going to jump on that wagon, fast!"

"When did you figure all this out? Because of the lean-burn thing?"

"No. When I was about fifteen and living in Hell with drunk parents. I was four blocks away from affluence you couldn't believe. Los Angeles, you know. I lived by being a thief and con artist, but saw how it was, in a lot of ways, a better life than the rich bitches. Through it all, I saw where I wanted my values to be. I didn't need a lot of things I didn't want or need to show up the neighbors. A friend and I had one very solid base for our scams: You don't scam anyone who can't afford it.

"The lean-burn invention started out as a scam,

turned into a real project, then ended as a scam. The oil companies could damned well afford it.

"This is my dream. I'm living in it because I saw how empty things are."

"Wha...! The lean-burn is a scam?! We tested it! It works!"

"And requires alloys that will stand stresses we do not have yet. Maybe they can be invented, but what works now is, as they say, prohibitively expensive. If they find something, it will be too late. We have the energy thing that just got its patent pending. It will knock the reason for that out of the picture."

Hallworthy almost squealed, shook his head, and made a very tired, wry grin. "Want to tell me something about your newest invention?"

"The light thing? Why would you care?"

"What?"

"I couldn't resist. Newest invention. Last week, not when I applied for the patent."

Hallworthjy laughed. "Don't make me like you. It's bad for business to fall into that trap."

"It gives you all the energy you can possibly use, free, in the form of electricity. It is cheap to produce. I haven't tested how long it will last, but what I have researched suggests it will perform to specs for a minimum of ten years. It may last a lot longer than that. I've designed the optimum size, so a hook-up to an inverter can be standardized.

As the patent says, it's output is fourteen volts. The ampere output is increased in a sort of direct ratio to ... another feature.

"A one square meter panel will supply enough power for basics, such as lights, refrigeration, TV or such. Two panels add air conditioning and such. Three can charge your car and so forth. A luxurious house with a pool and that kind of crap can run on four panels. A hotel can run six standard suites on one panel.

"The panel is a square meter by four centimeters thick and weighs nine pounds. It and an inverter/converter can be put in an eighteen inch wide closet.

"The panel costs about seventy five dollars to produce, but mass production will reduce that to about fifty, I suppose. They will sell for three hundred eighty five dollars, complete with the converter/inverter. A very good converter sells for less than a hundred bucks, retail."

"Such a thing would be easily worth two thousand dollars! Ten years of free electricity for two thousand is a *bargain*!"

"It will sell for three hundred eighty five dollars plus transportation, that will be very little. A truckload from LA to New York would cost about forty cents per panel. Cover all such costs and sell for three eighty nine ninety nine or something. The truck would carry four thousand units. The retailer gets a hundred bucks per unit, I get a hundred bucks a unit, the producer gets fifty. New York, the city, will initially need about a hundred trucks. That's twenty million from one city to the producer. We're talking about twenty five billion a year, just from the US. Other countries, it goes to two trillion a year for the first two years, then should level at about seven hundred billion a year from then on."

"And you will be able to buy a dozen Bill Gates in three months."

"No, I'll pay for real health care for all the third world people and all the poor anywhere. I'll still have a few billion to use for other projects."

"You're an idiot! You could have it all!"

"To what purpose?"

"What?"

"What should I do with ten or two trillion dollars a year? Eat it? I have exactly the life I want, right here. It costs about seven or eight hundred a month. A couple thousand for my research materials.

"What else would I want?"

"I don't think that deeply. It's not my nature."

"No. It's mine. I won't live a life with no meaning, and I'll leave this world with a legacy."

Hallworthy looked thoughtful for a couple of minute, then said, "What is this drink? It's absolutely delicious!"

"Guanabana chicha. It is good, isn't it? It also cures cancer, or prevents it, anyhow. You can combine that kind of thing, you know."

They chatted for more than an hour, then Hallworthy left.

Harry wasn't fooled by that act – at least the part that was an act. He went back to his lab and checked the hidden cameras. He picked up the four bugs the man left around the place, then went to the beach to turn off the tiny relay stations for them, then to behind the house to remove the bomb planted there under a large fig bush. He put the bomb on a little raft and sent it down the creek to the ocean, where it would go out three miles and sink the bomb in almost a mile depth of water. He was sure it wasn't nuclear, but they wouldn't be able to set it off there, anyhow.

He went to the house, where Maria had a fantastic dinner of crab-stuffed garlic shrimp.

Maria told him, in the morning, that she was sure she was pregnant.

Well, it was a good time for that, too! He would have someone to leave his legacy to!

Harry Andrews. founder of the Harry Andrews Food for the World Trust, teased at his twelve year old daughter. His fourteen year old son was coming from the beach carrying a large lobster (called a langosta here). His wife, Maria, called that Lou was on the phone.

He went in to greet his old friend.

"Just wanted to call to say 'Happy forty third birthday!' It's kind of a charge to be able to call the richest person in the world to chat."

Harry laughed. "How is the foundation going? Did you solve that thing in Africa, where the chiefs were stealing everything from their people and watching them starve?"

"Mutuki, Bramhas, Cototha. They all had fatal accidents, it seems. Nahimi and Green – an African tribal chief with a name like Green? – had heart attacks. Their hearts were attacked with a few ounces of brass jacketed lead. The food was then delivered and passed out. Med is requesting a ton of Artemisia from Panamá to stop a serious parasite infestation.

"We were able to help with that flood thing. We had a ship fairly close. We flew in meds and food.

Threw up a couple thousand shelters. We have that down to a science. Twenty directors and the people put them up in an hour.

"The oil companies have sheared a lot of their production and pay the sheiks and whoever about ten percent of what they got five years ago, and still they produce millions of barrels more than the world can use.

"A lot more of those sell-out politicians have been convicted. In the US, congressmen get a fixed salary, no perks, no bonuses, must be present a defined part of the time, and know that, if they are caught taking a bribe, they will serve a minimum of four years, not in a fancy hotel. In a prison with the very ones they preyed on.

"In other words, the new normal. The world was ready for a change and you came at just the right time.

"Do you want to spend twenty two billion on an idea for a spaceship that will operate on that old zero theory you told people you based your sling on?"

"Will it work?"

"Tests seem to say so. It uses microwaves to produce some kind of electrical drive. It will depend on a near source, such as the sun, for the first few cycles, then will be moving at such a rate that the lower concentrations can be used to accelerate more. It should be moving at three quarters lightspeed by the time it reaches Pluto's orbit. It will then take a few weeks to exceed lightspeed. We don't know from that point.

"Didn't you say that zero theory had something in it that would cut the time in half – or something?"

"If they're working from that, they have it already installed. I don't see how they could reach that velocity that soon without it. They have to also have the gyroscopic effect to stop inertial effects on any passengers. Lots of new technology that won't fuck up the world. Go for it."

They chatted awhile more, then Lou rang off. Maria called that she was going to fix the lobster Pepper (his son. They called him Pepper) caught for dinner. Lobster chowder.

They lived the life they wanted. The wealthiest man in the world, as far as money went, felt he was the wealthiest man in the world in his family and how they lived. Their closest friends on the island were the people on the island. Their children were being raised the way the island people were raised, with responsibility. They had both worked the same as the others on the island from when they were eight years old. They had responsibilities around the house when they were three or four. They were always in contact with their parents until they were three or four and most of the time until they were eight or nine, and still a lot more than in any so-called civilized place. They were wanted and loved and knew it, so were secure.

They were healthy, which added a lot.

Harry thought of something about that, so called Lou.

"Lou. The sterility bit. What happened with that? Is it reversible?"

Just three years ago it became obvious all over the world that the children were sterile. More than seventy percent of them. It was traced to a vaccination program and the use of certain genetically modified foods, with a possibility the attempts to control the climate added to it.

"No. There are some two thousand people under indictment for that. Most of them the wealthiest people on the planet. The conspiracy theorists were right about that part. A lot of them are on an island with a fortress designed to ward off a nuclear attack. They built it fifteen years ago, so there's no way they can deny that it was some kind of planned thing to control population.

"Hare, we did need population control, and it was the most humane way to have that, but I still can't go along with it."

"That's two of us. We can't do anything about it now, but you can bet those people's children didn't get the doses or whatever."

"That mentality is the last that should be the ones

to take over the world. They will have to stay sealed in that mausoleum they built. They thought of everything, it seems."

"Except that they can't take over anything from there. All they can hope for is to stay alive. Two generations and they can maybe get by, seeing all of the originals will be dead."

"Not necessarily. A lot of the life extension things work, and they have a few big drug research company executives and major scientists out there with them. There's supposed to be the most modern medical research facility on the Earth there. They plan to live for centuries and to come out as some kind of rulers, I'd say."

"They're locked into the idea of a static society that will depend on their supposed wealth to continue. They're mental dinosaurs.

"Lou, what kind of energy generation do they have?"

"Probably a few old generators and maybe nuclear, but mostly your crap."

"Can they survive without the, as you call it, crap?"

"Well, if they have nuclear, they could handle it pretty well for a long time. That would depend on them having someone who knows how to handle a nuclear reactor. I don't think they will have, seeing it would necessarily be a backup system."

"I want a damned powerful microwave generator

and beamed broadcast antenna. There's a little something about my system they don't know."

"Ahhh! Some kind of...?"

"Some kind of instability in one layer of the converter assembly."

Harry set the wavelength and turned on the microwave generator with the big parabolic antenna focused on the island on the horizon.

"Will it cook them, or what?"

"Not that. You wouldn't feel it in any way if you're more than a few hundred meters from the antenna. It's like the waves that run the system, just a different conformation. Those are going through you all the time. The system can neutralize normal levels."

"But abnormal levels?"

"Will alter the catalyst to where it will vaporize the transfer layer. Bummer!"

After about ten minutes, Harry turned off the generator and said they could go home at any time they wanted. Like now.

"They'll fire up the generators."

"And run out of fuel in a few days. They can't have a whole lot on the island. If they run out of fuel in a year, it will do."

"Then go to nuclear?"

"I studied about everyone there. They don't have anyone qualified to run a nuclear plant big enough to serve the whole place. I'd say they have to shut down the research facility."

"But that will be automatic failure!"

"That, or reduce their population drastically."

Lou giggled. "Now, who will choose who has to go?"

They did a high five and turned toward the shore and home.

"Well, it's been four years. Anything from the island?" Harry asked Lou, who was visiting with a boyfriend. Lou had studied some of the life extension, took care of himself, and looked, acted and felt like he was twenty years younger than he was.

"Not much. We found an internet site that may be from there, where they communicate with a few people. A few people in the families of the people out there. There was some kind of big shakeup or something a little over three years ago. If we understand their code, some kind of virus or something killed more than six hundred."

"So. They had to solve their own population problem. Predictable."

"They had a lot more fuel for the generators than we knew. I think they're about done with that. They tried to get some platinum catalytic converter beads sent, but we stopped that.

"Trying to fix their panels?"

"I'd say. The nuclear is their last hope."

"They're trying to get someone who knows the science out there. Guarantee a million dollars gold if their problem is solved."

"So they know there is a world currency. They would, having the net to keep up with things."

"I'm surprised they haven't tried to contact you."

"Maybe they have. I haven't checked the old e-mails in nearly a year. Why bother when we can talk on the phone or vocals on the net so easily. I'll check."

They went out to the lab and turned on the computer. Harry checked all four of his e-mails. Two of them had requests for information. One was a rant about unfairness when all they were trying to do was save the world from massive starvation. One was more direct.

Mr. Andrews - I represent a group of people who are in dire straits due to a couple of bad business decisions. We are, of course, on Paradise Island, which has become Hell Island.

We cannot survive here much longer, as I'm as certain you know. We can only suppose you included a fail-safe in your inverter systems. I can report that it was 100% effective.

I really can't think of a way to approach anyone who would feel that my pitiful six billion pounds is, as the saying goes, pocket change

However, it is the only thing I know.

Several people here will join with me. People as successful as am I in business.

Mr. Andrews, if you can get us off this island and to reasonable safety, we will pay you a total of six hundred billion pounds. In gold, which is the medium we brought.

Number 10091

Harry shook his head. He answered: *If there is one thing in this universe that does not interest me, it is money. I would think that is plain to an idiot.*

You are in a trap you built. If I cared, one way or the other, I have a weapon that your silly nuclear-proof fortress would fall to in five minutes.

Enjoy the fruits of your labors. I will enjoy a guanabana chicha, personally, picked from a tree about thirty feet away from where I am at this moment.

HA

He sent it and went to check on his latest experiment: a better way to grow okra.

The computer dinged. He saw he had a return on his e-mail.

Mr. Andrews – people here are insane! We are at each others throats, casting blame about. Some are wanting to join in a suicide pact! It's crazy! Two people were shot. One was strangled. Four are locked in the medical laboratories. I don't know what's happening! They were the ones who wanted a suicide pact! They're crazy! I think they plan to cause some kin

That was the end of it. Whatever happened, the writer had some way to hit "send."

Harry turned off the machine and went to walk on the beach with Maria.

The next morning Harry went to the lab. He turned on the computer and sent a query to the e-mail on the island. It was about an hour later when he got an e-mail return.

Mr. Andrews, perhaps you will remember me. Evander Hallworthy.

I am the last one alive here. Sendero Pencero made some kind of thing in the medical laboratory that killed everyone. Some kind of gas. It was not cyanide, as I know the odor of that.

I am alive solely because I was in an isolation chamber to escape just that kind of thing.

I heard them planning, you see. I thought they would kill several people and try to arrange some kind of deal with all their money, such as what they tried with you. I knew you would not.

It is possible they planned that, but the gas was faster and more deadly than they knew.

Be that as it may, I am here. You may send someone for me. I was never a part of sterilizing people or that kind of thing. I was only after a way to make more money. I have learned the stupidity of that too late.

I swear to you that I was not involved in more than business. The plots and plans of many were not known by myself. I swear this to you. I would never do that, under any circumstances. I can see why and how it would become what it became.

I am at a loss as to what else to do.

Vandy

Harry sighed and wrote: *I will inform the authorities and will state to the world that I believe you were not part of that. I don't know if I have the influence to change anything beyond that.*

Hare

He called the CIA. He had the number for the top man. It would be out of his hands from then.

We make the world we have to inhabit. He couldn't logically understand why so many made the worlds they would have to live in with the idea they were exempt from consequences.

Well, what would he like for lunch?

Four days later he got a call from Hallworthy. They had given him a lie detector test and found that he, indeed, had no knowledge of the sterility thing and that he would never have agreed to such measures. His funds were seized, as were all those on the island, to be used for medical research and treatment. The funds were sufficient to guarantee the treatments worldwide for twenty nine years. He was released. Imprisoning him would serve no purpose, and he was innocent of most of the charges they could bring.

Harry wished him well. He would have to find a new niche.

"Harry was a rare person, a person who came from nothing and made himself into everything for a lot of people, me among them," Lou said to the gathering of some of the island's people and several reporters. "He judged no one. We all judge him as being one of the most worthwhile people to have ever lived.

"He wished for nothing like this for a funeral, and I feel guilty for being a part of it. He always said to dig a hole and toss him in it or dump him at sea, where he would at least feed the crabs. He knew he wasn't immortal. He knew that we arrive here with nothing and take nothing with us when we leave. He knew that one day his time would be up, as it is for all of us. Let his lifeless body serve some purpose. His legacy was what mattered,

"Would that the bunch of us here, combined, could leave a tenth of what his legacy will be.

"We compromised. His ashes I hereby toss into the sea to fertilize the algae that will in turn feed many forms of life and will convert carbon dioxide to life-giving oxygen.

"If ever a man lived who deserved continuation of his stay in paradise, it was Hare. He nor I believe in gods, but, if there is one, consider what Hare was. If you exist, he will be in that paradise.

"Farewell, my friend. You made the world better for all of us." He spread the ashes onto the stream where it met the Caribbean. Everyone went home. He bid the last of them "Farewell!" and went inside, where Harry was sitting with Maria and his son and daughter.

"Maybe they'll let me have some peace now," he said. "Whose ashes were those?"

"Some crud where we burned off the cashew husks," Pepper said. "Well, now for the important stuff, like how will I handle the trillions I inherited?"

"I gave it all to the fund. You're left with just my personal emergency account. You and your sister and Maria will only have about three million apiece, so you'd better get off your lazy asses and learn to make a living!"

"Well, if we have to, we have to," Salt, his daughter, said.

"What's for dinner?" Harry asked.

Maria replied, "Just some gumbo. That strain of okra you came up is really a winner!"

They chatted and played into the night. In the morning Lou went back to Barbados.

"Guess I'll need a new project. Wonder what would happen if my weapon was fired into a small lump of uranium or such. Would the compression factor make it go critical?" Harry asked himself.

"You won't do that test with me here!" he answered himself.

C. D. Moulton's works are available on most major outlets as printed or e-books. CD writes the CD Grimes, PI, mysteries, the Det. Lt. Nick Storie mysteries, the Clint Faraday mysteries, the Flight of the Maita science fiction series, books on orchid culture and many others of many types. Mystery, adventure, intrigue, science fiction, humor, fantasy, paranormal, mild erotica, and factual.

9 7 9 8 2 1 5 7 8 2 4 4 6